A NOTE TO PARENTS

Reading Aloud with Your Child

Research shows that reading books aloud is the single most valuable support parents can provide in helping children learn to read.

- Be a ham! The more enthusiasm you display, the more your child will enjoy the book.
- Run your finger underneath the words as you read to signal that the print carries the story.
- Leave time for examining the illustrations more closely; encourage your child to find things in the pictures.
- Invite your youngster to join in whenever there's a repeated phrase in the text.
- Link up events in the book with similar events in your child's life.
- If your child asks a question, stop and answer it. The book can be a means to learning more about your child's thoughts.

Listening to Your Child Read Aloud

The support of your attention and praise is absolutely crucial to your child's continuing efforts to learn to read.

- If your child is learning to read and asks for a word, give it immediately so that the meaning of the story is not interrupted. DO NOT ask your child to sound out the word.
- On the other hand, if your child initiates the act of sounding out, don't intervene.
- If your child is reading along and makes what is called a miscue, listen for the sense of the miscue. If the word "road" is substituted for the word "street," for instance, no meaning is lost. Don't stop the reading for a correction.
- If the miscue makes no sense (for example, "horse" for "house"), ask your child to reread the sentence because you're not sure you understand what's just been read.
- Above all else, enjoy your child's growing command of print and make sure you give lots of praise. *You are your child's first teacher — and the most important one. Praise from you is critical for further risk-taking and learning.*

— Priscilla Lynch
Ph.D., New York University
Educational Consultant

To Margaret and Jordan Mathis,
and Natalie James
— A.S.M.

For Julie Hannah,
a mom in a million.
— J.H.

Text copyright © 1996 by Angela Shelf Medearis
Illustrations copyright © 1996 by Joan Holub
All rights reserved. Published by Scholastic Inc.
HELLO READER!, CARTWHEEL BOOKS, and the CARTWHEEL BOOKS logo
are registered trademarks of Scholastic Inc.

No part of this publication may be reproduced in whole or in part, or stored in a retrieval system, or transmitted in any form or by any means, electronic, mechanical, photocopying, recording, or otherwise, without written permission of the publisher. For information regarding permission, write to Scholastic Inc., 555 Broadway, New York, NY 10012.

Library of Congress Cataloging-in-Publication Data
Medearis, Angela Shelf, 1956–
    The 100th day of school / by Angela Shelf Medearis; illustrated
by Joan Holub.
    p. cm. — (Hello reader. Level 2)
    "Cartwheel Books."
    Summary: The children learn 100 spelling words, plant 100 seeds, bake
100 cookies, and "do everything the 100 way" to celebrate this special day.
    ISBN 0-590-25944-X
    [1. Schools — Fiction. 2. Counting — Fiction. 3. Stories in rhyme.] I. Holub,
Joan, ill. II. Title. III. Series.
PZ8.3.M551155Aaf   1996
[E] — dc20   95-13214
                                                                  CIP
                                                                  AC

24 23 22 21 20 19 18 17 16   8 9/9 0 1/0

Printed in the U.S.A.   24

First Scholastic printing, January 1996

The 100th Day of School

by Angela Shelf Medearis
Illustrated by Joan Holub

Hello Reader! — Level 2

SCHOLASTIC INC.

New York   Toronto   London   Auckland   Sydney

In school, we work,
we learn, we play.

We count up to
a special day.

We mark the calendar
as a rule.
Today is it —
the 100th day of school!

On the 100th day,
we shout hooray!
Then we do everything
the 100 way.

We count to 100

and from 100
to one.

Saying 100 numbers
is so much fun!

100 99 98 97 96 95 94 93 92 91 90 89 88 87 86 85 84 83 82 81 80 79 78 77 76 75 74 73 72 71 70 69 68 67 66 65 64 63 62 61 60 59 58 57 56 55 54 53 52 51 50 49 48 47 46 45 44 43 42 41 40 39 38 37 36 35 34 33 32 31

We learn 100 words
for the spelling bee.

We put 100 bows
on a little tree.

We jump 100 times
to a jumping song.

We draw a snake
100 inches long.

TIPTON ELEMENTARY PRIMARY

We put 100 cans
in the recycling bin,

and 100 newspapers
in ten stacks of ten.

We plant 100 seeds.
There are two in each cup.
Plants need sun.
We line the fifty cups up.

We make special hats
with 100 stars.

We take 100 pennies
from our penny jars.

We buy 100 balloons
at the store.
There are twenty-five of us.
We each get four.

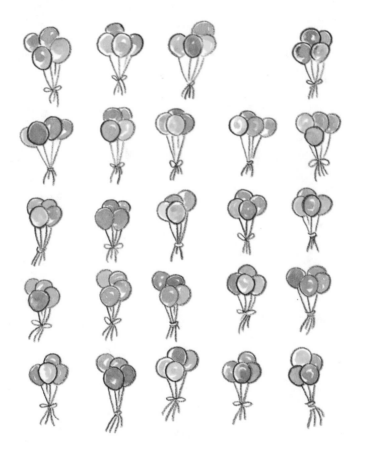

We bake 100 cookies
on five pans of twenty.
We can all share
because we have plenty.

Now it's time for our party!
Hip! Hip! Hooray!
We've been in school
100 days!